DATE DUE

CASTLE OF DARKNESS

CHOOSE YOUR OWN
NIGHTMARE...
titles in Large-Print Editions:

NIGHTMARE...

CASTLE OF DARKNESS
BY R. A. MONTGOMERY

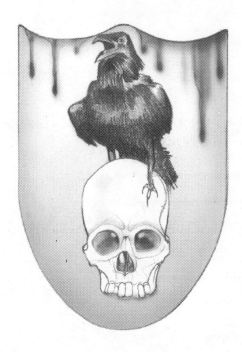

ILLUSTRATED BY BILL SCHMIDT

Gareth Stevens Publishing
MILWAUKEE

J

c. 1

For a free color catalog describing Gareth Stevens' list of high-quality books, call 1-800-542-2595 (USA) or 1-800-461-9120 (Canada). Gareth Stevens' Fax: (414) 225-0377.

Library of Congress Cataloging-in-Publication Data

Montgomery, R. A.
    Castle of darkness / by R. A. Montgomery ; illustrated by
  Bill Schmidt.
        p. cm. — (Choose your own nightmare)
      Summary: The reader's decisions control the course of an adventure
  in which three friends win a trip to an English castle where they
  become trapped in the dungeons.
      ISBN 0-8368-1513-0 (lib. bdg.)
      1. Plot-your-own stories. [1. Castles—Fiction. 2. Adventure
  and adventurers—Fiction. 3. Plot-your-own stories.] I. Schmidt, Bill,
  ill. II. Title. III. Series.
  PZ7.M7684Cas   1996
  [Fic]—dc20   95-39819

This edition first published in 1996 by
Gareth Stevens Publishing
1555 North RiverCenter Drive, Suite 201
Milwaukee, Wisconsin 53212 USA

CHOOSE YOUR OWN NIGHTMARE™ is a trademark of Bantam Doubleday Dell Books for Young Readers, a division of Bantam Doubleday Dell Publishing Group, Inc.

Printed in the United States of America

1 2 3 4 5 6 7 8 9 99 98 97 96

CASTLE OF DARKNESS

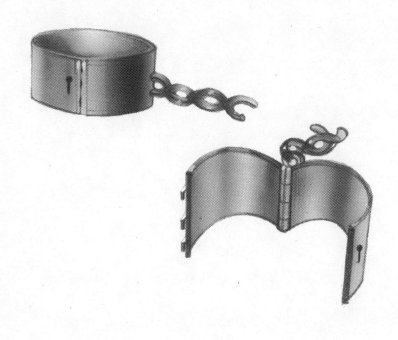

WARNING!

You have probably read books where scary things happen to people. Well, in *Choose Your Own Nightmare,* you're right in the middle of the action. The scary things are happening to you!

Visiting an English castle is a dream come true . . . until you end up trapped in the deep dungeons that lie below!

Fortunately, while you're reading along, you'll have chances to decide what to do. Whenever you make a decision, turn to the page shown. The thrills and chills that happen to you next will depend on your choices.

So make sure to choose carefully—or else you may be calling a dungeon . . . home.

Josh Mitchell is your best friend, not counting Megan Carullo, who could also be called your best friend. The three of you met at a skateboarding center several years ago and you all go to the same school.

You are pretty lucky to have them for best friends. You have a lot of fun hanging out together, going skateboarding—even doing homework is fun when they're around.

The three of you love castles and their dungeons. Not that you've ever been to any. But you all worked together last year on a social studies project about castles. That did it!

"It would have been so cool to have lived back then," Megan sighed as you flipped through one of your library books about castles. She thinks it must have been great back in the days of tournaments and pageants. "All those jousts and stuff," she said.

"Yeah," Josh agreed. "Back in the time of the knights of the Round Table."

Turn to page 2.

2

Josh is eleven years old. He's one of the wackiest—in the best sense of the word—kids you have ever met. Josh likes to try to wear his shoes backward so people think he's going instead of coming. His hair is shaved really short on the sides even though his parents hate it, and he can chew bubble gum and eat a cheeseburger at the same time and not get them confused! He's also a bit of a wise guy, which often gets you both into trouble.

Megan is a different kettle of fish, as your mom likes to say. Megan is eleven too. She is really smart. She's in all the advanced classes at school and she's always asking her teachers for extra work. Most kids try to get *out* of homework. Not Megan. And you can't even try to change her mind. She can argue the teeth out of a shark and sell them back to him without so much as blinking.

Not only is she good in school, Megan is also a super gymnast. She's always flipping and tumbling—basically showing off—in gym class. She wants to be in the Olympics someday. But she has a terrible diet, and her mom says too much pizza will hold her back.

Go on to the next page.

Megan lives in a small house on the edge of town with her grandfather and mother. Her dad left right after she was born. She comes to your house almost every day. She sometimes says that she wants to run away and join a circus. Josh thinks that's a pretty good idea; you aren't so sure. Megan listens to you, because you're a little bit older (three months) and, she thinks, wiser.

Josh has four sisters, so he spends most of his time with you. Having so many sisters can be a big pain, he tells you. He gets blamed for stuff he didn't do, he doesn't get credit for doing the dishes when he does them, and he always has to wait in line for the bathroom.

The three of you have formed your own secret club. Since you are a little bit older, and because the secret club was your idea from the start, you are the head of it. Besides, it meets at *your* house. The only trouble is that you don't have any real secrets. Who'd want to know your dad's unlisted telephone number or your mom's secret recipe for spaghetti sauce? Your club doesn't even have a name. It's *that* secret.

Turn to page 4.

4

You spend a lot of time at meetings of your club discussing castles and dungeons and knights. Megan thinks that there were probably some great knights who were women. There probably were, you agree. Who could tell under all that armor?

You love the thought of knights and huge battles fought outside castle walls, you love the idea of bad people being locked deep in dungeons beneath castles, and you love even more the thought of rescuing good people who have been locked deep in the dungeons by evil ones. It's your dream to go to England and Scotland, to visit the real thing.

Sometimes dreams *shouldn't* come true.

One sunny summer afternoon, Megan appears at your porch door with a look on her face that can mean only one of two things: trouble or excitement. You don't even bother flipping a coin; somehow you know it's trouble.

"Well, what is it this time?" you ask.

"Lighten up!" she exclaims. "You'll never believe it!"

Go on to the next page.

You're not in a great mood today. Your mom has made you clean out your room and it's taken you three hours.

"What? I don't have all day," you say.

"So*rry*," she says, emphasizing the last syllable. "I had an opportunity for you . . . but if you aren't interested, then I guess me and old Josh will have to go alone." Megan turns as if to leave and then slows down and waits.

"Go where?"

"Josh and I entered a magazine contest to identify four little-known castles in England and Scotland. By name and place. We had only pieces of pictures to go on."

"Big deal."

"We W-O-N." Megan twists the letters in her mouth like spaghetti, getting all the juice and flavor from them.

"Won what?"

"Three tickets to England, travel money for one week, and . . . we get to stay in one of the castles!" Megan starts leaping around the porch. "Ravensford Castle. And it's totally cool. It's been closed to the public till now. Last year it was opened up to tourists."

Turn to page 48.

6

Suddenly you find your head spinning. To your utter amazement, you're rushing through a tunnel in time and space to a hole of light that accelerates in a whirl of speed.

Thump! You land on the ground with a horrible whack to your backside.

"Where am I?" you mumble, standing up. Josh and Megan are right beside you. "Guys!" you say. "What happened? How did you get here?"

Josh shrugs. "Beats me. We just arrived too. Last thing I remember, we were trapped in a tiny dungeon, then—boom! We're here."

"Quit talking," says Megan. "Look!"

In front of you are a group of ordinary-looking people, but they seem frozen in action.

"Are they alive?" you ask.

"Should we try and communicate with these things? They look like statues," Josh says.

"Might as well," Megan replies, stepping forward to a knight.

"Don't touch me," he whispers.

"Why not?" she asks.

"Because I'll break or turn to dust. I'm very old, you know. But I can help you."

Turn to page 18.

"Yes, I thought you might like to play my game," Ranny says. "It is a simple one that has been played many times over the centuries. Win, and you and your friends go free. Lose—well, then you'll just be here for the next hundred years or. so."

"How do you play?" you whisper, fearing the reply.

"Simple, really. A child's game, you might say," Ranny tells you happily. He rubs his hands together.

"I'm all ears," you say, trying to sound brave.

"Good. Here's how we play. It's a special kind of hide-and-seek. You see, I hide your friends in odd places. You seek them. If you find them and—this is the important part—you are able to free them, then all is fine and well. They earn their freedom, and I lose."

"What happens if I don't find them?" you ask.

Turn to page 15.

8

You feel the same sense of a mist descending over you that you experienced reading your E-mail back home. *How does he know what I'd like?* you think.

The old man stands there, waiting.

"I want to go!" says Josh.

"Me too," says Megan. "Please, Aunt Nestra? We'll be fine."

Nestra looks at the old man. "You do work for the castle?" she asks.

"Longer than anyone else," he says, toying with his pruning shears.

Nestra faces the three of you. "First, we have to check in. And then get something to eat. If you want to explore around the castle after dinner, I guess it's all right."

"Yes!" Megan and Josh shout in unison.

"What about you?" Nestra asks you.

You're not sure what to do. You want to hang out with your friends, but this old man is kind of creepy.

If you decide to go with Josh, Megan, and the old man, turn to page 17.

If you decide to stay put at the castle, turn to page 56.

You nod. Then, all of a sudden, you feel an icy hand on your neck!

"Hello. Sorry I'm late. Something came up," says the old man.

"That's okay," you say, your heart pounding. He's wearing dark pants and a loose, flowing tunic. "What's your name, by the way?" you ask.

Looking at you as though you were a butterfly on a pin waiting to be put into his collection, the old man answers, "Some call me Caxton, others just the Old One. You can call me Sir Ranald."

"Sir? Are you a knight?" Josh asks. "Like one of the knights of the Round Table?"

"You might say I was, at least in another time and another place. Pay it no heed. Just call me Ranny, if that pleases you." He shuffles a bit, looking impatient to get going.

"Righto," you say, getting into the feel of being in jolly Olde England. "We'll follow you," you say. The three of you walk down onto one of the gravel paths that lead away from the castle, with Ranny in front.

Turn to page 44.

"Yeah," says Megan. "We saw where the horse stables are, and the rooms where they store a lot of the old armor. We even got to try some of it on!"

"What about the dungeons?" you ask. You feel a bit jealous that they had so much fun.

Josh frowns. "The old guy didn't want to show us them without you."

"Guess he doesn't want to give the dungeon tour twice," says Megan. "So you've got to come tomorrow night."

"Okay," you agree.

Nestra has been dabbing her sweater with water. "Time for bed, everyone," she says, stretching.

It doesn't take long to get into your big bed. Sleep hits you like a hammer blow.

Near two o'clock in the morning, when the moon is slivered by clouds, a scratching sound at the door disturbs your sleep.

"Josh?" you call out. No answer. "Megan?" Still no answer. The scratching continues.

"Who's there?" you ask. "What do you want?"

Turn to page 40.

"I'm afraid not. But we do have some suits of armor that you can try on. They're not real —but they look just like the real thing."

"Oh. Okay," says Josh. You can tell he's disappointed—he'd rather try the real one on.

You and Josh each have your own rooms, while Megan is sharing with Nestra. After you put your things away, you head down to the dining room for dinner.

"Have you changed your mind?" Josh asks, wiping his mouth on his sleeve. It's now 7:45. Your dinner—roast beef and chips, as the English call french fries—was really good.

You shake your head. "No. I want to stay here and relax. Maybe do some reading about the castle or something."

"Okay. But don't say we didn't ask you," says Megan. She gives you a wave, and she and Josh tear out of the room.

"Can I get you anything else?" asks Clara, your waitress. She's also the maid.

"Maybe another spot of tea," says Nestra.

"Nothing for me," you say. Clara begins to walk away, then stops. "Have you met young Tommy yet?" she asks you.

Turn to page 70.

12

"Let's not get rude, or else I can get really nasty," the voice continues. "Want to see my face?"

"Not really," you reply.

"Well, you're going to, like it or not."

The door swings open.

"I'm here. And don't forget that I warned you not to come!" The speaker is wearing a jean jacket and pants, but over his head is an ancient helmet with slits for eyes. He's about your size. "If you're ready, I am," the person says, and slowly reaches up to remove the helmet. Off it comes.

Horror of all horrors! Where there should be a nose and lips and eyes is a flat white wooden plate. Tears stain the wood where the eyes should be. You rear back in disgust and fear. Whatever happened to this person? Why is he picking on you—and how did he know about you back in the States?

"Welcome to England. Are you ready?" His voice is muffled—the plate makes it hard to hear him.

Turn to page 29.

"A real joust?" you ask, dreading Ranny's reply.

"Yes. You are a brave one. We'll have a tournament. It will start with a joust and go on to single armed combat. I hope you're good with swords."

Your mind reels with the horror of your situation. If only King Arthur were around, you think. But wait a minute. Isn't Arthur the once and future king? If things are this out of hand, couldn't there also be truth to the legend? Couldn't Arthur come back and help you now?

Ranny puts on a red and yellow robe. He is wearing tights, and his shoes are long and pointed.

"The tournament begins!" he shouts. You hear a trumpet blow.

Turn to page 62.

"That's where it gets interesting," Ranny says, rubbing his dry, wrinkled hands in macabre glee. "You see, your friends will be—how can I say this kindly?—in precarious positions. Time is of the essence. Find them, free them, and on to a tour of the old castle. Don't find them and don't free them, and, well . . . they'll get to stay here a long, long time.

A shiver runs down your spine. "Look. If you'll just tell me where they are right now, I promise I won't report you. We'll pretend none of this ever happened," you say. Your voice cracks a little bit.

Ranny shakes his head. "Oh, but it *is* happening," he says, smiling. "Just as it has happened every year for the past seven hundred years."

"You are a sicko!" you scream.

"Perhaps, but it's all in the way you look at it. Point of view, that's what it is. On with the game."

"How long do I have?" you ask.

Turn to page 65.

16

You need to get help. Turning, you race across the drawbridge, your sneakers thudding on the damp wood. It's really hard to see now. Not only is it pitch-black, but rolls of fog have come in off the sea, making everything cloudy and dreamlike.

Realizing that nothing is coming after you, you slow down. *Okay, you tell yourself,* struggling to stay calm. *All I have to do is find the main entrance to the castle. I'll go get Nestra, and we'll call the police. Josh and Megan will be fine.* Your heart pounding, you start off.

How can you not find the castle entrance, you ask yourself. It's big. It's a castle! Stumbling forward, you squint, trying to make out something, anything, in the fog. Nothing.

"I've *got* to find it!" you shout in frustration as you bend down to tie your shoelace.

Galump. Galump. In an instant, you are on your feet. What is that noise?

Galump. Galump. It's getting closer! It sounds like . . . like a horse! Frantically, you try to decide which way to turn. You don't want to get run over—and you don't want the ghost knights to get you, either!

Turn to page 76.

"Okay, I'll go," you say.

The old man nods. "I'll meet you at the castle's front entrance at eight P.M.," he says. He turns his back on you and starts trimming the bush again.

"Come on," says Nestra, as she walks across the bridge that leads to the castle. You look down at the moat underneath. It's filled with murky, black water. You imagine former times when it was used as a first line of defense against attackers. The portcullis—the iron grating that hangs over the doorway—is up, allowing people to enter.

Josh pushes open the castle door. The doorknobs are shaped like gargoyles. They're pretty creepy, you think. The door is made of dark brown wood and extremely heavy. It gives a slight creak when it opens. Above the door is a coat of arms—a raven perched on a skull. You guess that's how the castle got its name.

Turn to page 63.

"Who are you?" you ask, amazed that you have a living ally here in this temple of doom.

"Sir Archibald the Brave. Thirteenth century. A knight-errant. I was captured here and escaped, only to wander the halls of this castle for the remainder of my life. I appear every hundred years on a quest, hoping to serve the likes of you. Evil things have happened here. I can help stop them."

"Good. Because we need help," you say.

"Follow me. I know the way out. It takes at least three of us, and now we have four."

The knight tells you that you're in the deepest depths of the castle. He clanks a bit but is surprisingly agile in his armor for his extended age. The route he takes leads you to a back stairway in the far recesses of the castle that ascends to the ancient kitchens, where giant feasts were often prepared in the castle's heyday. Tournaments were held, jousts were performed, and life was happy in the thirteenth century, Archibald tells you, before the "evil days," when Ranny's ancestors took their unjust revenge on the owners of the castle.

Turn to page 28.

This must be another one of Tommy's *un-funny* jokes. You never would have gone with him if you'd known what a pain he was.

"This is definitely not funny!" you shout. "Come on—turn off the water!" you yell. But the water continues to rise.

You try to stay calm. "Don't panic," you whisper to yourself. This dumb kid is just joking around. The lights will come on any moment now, you think . . . you hope . . . you pray. Let him have his little joke. Maybe this is the initiation into the club of castle seekers. It's hot, it's damp, it's scary, it's uncomfortable, it's miserable.

"Help!" you scream.

The water rises slowly but continually. Finally it fills the underground dungeons. You gasp and take in a huge gulp of water, your last breath. The castle has claimed yet another victim.

Josh and Megan search for you the following day. The local police and then Scotland Yard are called in, but you are never found. Tommy claims he never, ever saw you.

The End

20

"Don't be afraid—come in, come in," Ranny says.

Megan is already inside the courtyard. She turns to speak. "Hey, guys, it's great in here! Come on!"

That's when it happens!

From out of the shadows of the castle wall swoop two figures clad in the traditional garb of the knight going to battle: doublets, breast-plates, gauntlets, and helmets! They are completely silent—there is no sound of clanking, as you would have imagined.

"Whoa!" you say, stumbling backward. The knights look ready for battle. What if they're after *you*?

"Run for it!" you shout to Megan.

But she is busy nosing around and doesn't pay any attention. And where is Josh? He's gone!

Turn to page 33.

"Okay, let's go," Clytemnestra says after you get your luggage, leading the way to her car. Before long you are out on the road heading toward Clytemnestra's house, which is about an hour from Heathrow. It's pretty weird to be driving on the other side of the road. Clytemnestra's driving leaves a little to be desired, so you all hang on tight.

Nestra—that's her nickname—lives in a narrow brick house in a suburb of London.

"I guess jet lag is setting in," you tell Megan. You are very tired. She nods sleepily.

After a mug of hot chocolate, Nestra shows you each to your rooms and says goodnight. "Up early tomorrow!" she says, gently closing your door.

A night in London, a day on the road, and you finally find your way to the town of Last Momentum, right on the Scottish border. The air is sweet with the smell of summer flowers and warm, almost sultry. It is late afternoon, and you're all a little cramped from riding in Aunt Nestra's tiny car.

A small sign indicates the road to Ravensford Castle. "This is it!" shouts Megan.

Turn to page 74.

22

But how will you find Josh? It's pitch-black, huge, hot, and horrible. It's a dungeon of nightmares.

Hurriedly, you try to take off your armor. It's getting really hot inside, and very uncomfortable. But just as you get one of the gauntlets off, you hear the sound of footsteps on the stairway behind you. They're after you!

Your surroundings are so dark and frightening that you haven't the faintest idea where the sound of Josh's voice is coming from. It seems to well up all over the chamber of dungeons, as though broadcast from a set of quadraphonic speakers.

"Where are you?" you squeak.

"Here," is the reply.

There's no time to get the rest of your armor off. You stumble through the blackness of the upper chamber, slipping off the landing and onto another stairway. You feel closed in by the walls, by the stale, warm air, by the evil of hundreds of years past, when humans suffered and breathed their last in this very spot. You can hear them screaming, feel their pain, experience their terror.

Turn to page 59.

Then, without warning, the bulb extinguishes. Tommy's flashlight wavers and then goes out. A thin scream comes from your side, followed by silence.

"Are you scared?" comes Tommy's voice. He laughs.

"Where are you?" you shout. No reply.

The laughter repeats—shorter, more horrifying in its terror—and then stops again. It's almost ghoulish. You take a deep breath. It feels as if the room is getting hotter, and you hear running water.

Then you *feel* water. It covers the tips of your sneakers. It climbs your legs. It is cold and dark and slimy.

Turn to page 19.

The book is filled with all sorts of legends about knights, and also paintings of them. The people look odd to you—not at all like the paintings you have in your living room back home. In fact they look kind of spooky, with big heads and funny-shaped bodies. The stories are pretty good, though. You've read a lot of stories about knights, but the stories in this book are brand-new to you.

Suddenly your ears perk up. You hear a noise. It almost sounds as if someone is whispering your name.

"Who's there?" you say loudly. No answer. You try to concentrate on the book, but again you hear a noise. This time it sounds like someone moaning.

"Hello!" you say. You put your book down and get up.

If you decide to investigate, turn to page 32.

If you continue to read, turn to page 60.

26

But there is no reply. You follow your instincts and continue along the narrow corridor. Suddenly, you hear footsteps coming toward you. You stop and listen. It can't be Josh or Megan—they're trapped.

The footsteps are getting closer and closer. They sound heavy, like an adult's.

Ranny must be behind you! You press yourself up against the wall, hoping he'll pass by without seeing you. You realize that's not too likely.

You stick your head forward to hear better and—pow!—someone bangs into you.

"Look Ranny, you didn't give me enough time. You aren't playing fair. I—I—" you babble, standing up.

"Ranny who?" says a crisp English voice. Your eyes widen.

Turn to page 45.

The part of the castle the guests stay in is filled with great halls, roaring fireplaces, and steaming kitchens. It's quite different here. Here are only the dungeons.

Then you notice Ranny standing a few feet in front of you. He smiles, as benign and friendly as before. He looks like a harmless old man, hunched by age and possibly deformity. But there's definitely something creepy about him. You wish you had stayed with Nestra.

"So?" he says.

"So! So what is going on here?" you demand. "I want my friends back. And I want to go back to the *normal* part of the castle." You wrap your arms around yourself. "I promise I won't report you. But this isn't much fun. Deal?"

Turn to page 54.

"This way," says the knight. "Be very careful."

The kitchens are vast. The ancient hearths, where pots bubbled and roasts turned on iron spits, are filled only with memory and debris. Nothing at all like the clean, orderly kitchen the castle's bed-and-breakfast operates. Archibald skirts the huge vats where pigs were rendered for their fat. Rodents scurry away.

"Here we are," he says, pointing to a narrow window high in the wall. "Below this window is the moat. It used to be an escape route during the early wars. But it's too high for me. I need help. I can't swim."

"We'll help you," you say. But it's not an easy task, especially when you suspect Ranny is on his way!

Turn to page 78.

"For what?" you say, backing up.

"For your initiation," he says.

"What kind of initiation?" you ask anxiously.

"For membership in the Loyal Order of the Knights of Times Past. It's really a terrific group, and we know all about you and your interests. Got the info on you from some friends in America. One condition, though: You have to promise never to reveal our secrets or who we are. Agreed?" You nod.

The faceless knight removes the wooden plate. It's no knight—it's a kid about your age.

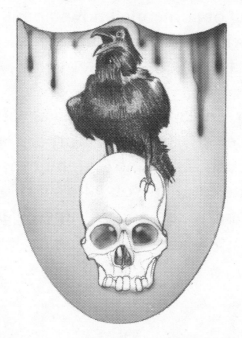

Turn to page 79.

30

Two days later, when you make a last check on your computer for E-mail, you find something that sends a mist over your happiness.

YOU WILL REGRET EVER THINKING ABOUT VISITING RAVENSFORD CASTLE. MARK THESE WORDS WELL. THERE IS A DUNGEON JUST FOR YOU. THERE IS NO SALVATION.

THE FACELESS KNIGHT

You stare at the screen, and then, without your even having touched a key, the message disappears. You check the computer, but nothing is wrong. Something has intervened. Something or someone knows about your fascination with castles. You know it's not a joke. The message has the ring of truth.

London, England! What a blast, you think as you arrive at Heathrow Airport and pass through customs. Aunt Clytemnestra is there to meet the three of you. She's got long, curly red hair and wears horn-rimmed glasses. You like her at once.

Turn to page 21.

"Finally!" Josh says. He's trying to act cool, but he can't hide the fact that he's terrified. Little beads of perspiration glisten on his fore-head.

The key to the chains is lying just out of their reach. Quickly you pick it up and unlock them.

"This way," Josh says, rubbing his wrists. "Megan and I were up there before. I think I know a way to escape."

"Lead the way," you reply, glad to have someone else make the decisions for now. But you don't relax for long.

In a few minutes you are in another large hall. It looks like an old ballroom. The floor is covered with black-and-white tiles. There's something strange about them. Some of the tiles are very small, about the size of your thumbnail. It is an odd, eccentric pattern. You get dizzy looking at it.

"Ahh!" Josh shrieks from the other side of the room. A thin silver cord is wrapped around his ankle, holding him in place.

"Josh! What's going on?" you ask, going over. You're careful not to get too close.

Turn to page 81.

You move away from the table. You aren't going to let a little whisper scare you. "Who is it?" you ask. The moaning is getting louder . . . and closer. You step closer to the door. In a flash, you whip it open, trying to gain the element of surprise on whoever is out there.

"What do you want?" you say, leaping into the hallway.

"Oh!" says a woman standing there. It's Nestra! "I was bringing you a cup of hot chocolate when I stumbled on the carpet. I'm afraid I spilled it all over myself," she says. She holds up the empty mug.

You recover your breath. "Did you burn yourself?" you ask.

"No, luckily. How's it going?"

You tell her about the interesting book you found. "But I think I'll finish it tomorrow," you add.

The two of you head back to the dining room, where you find Josh and Megan, back from their outing, gobbling up some cookies.

"It was so cool," Josh tells you. "This place is huge!"

Turn to page 10.

"Ranny!" you shriek. But the old man has disappeared, too.

The silent knights rush for you and Megan. Using your best moves from skateboarding and your beginner's karate class, you prepare to dodge them. But time is running out; they are closing in on you!

The sound of the portcullis coming slowly down penetrates your consciousness. There's still time to escape out the door and across the moat. But what about Megan and Josh? Can you leave them behind?

If you decide to run for it and get out of the castle, turn to page 35.

If you decide to stay and deal with the situation— after all, it might be harmless—turn to page 64.

34

You realize that if you want to see your friends alive again, you'd better do what he says.

"Okay, you want me to get others for your dungeons in exchange for Josh and Megan— you've got it," you say in a voice full of false courage. "No problem."

"Good. I knew from the beginning you would agree. Your ultimate rewards will be beyond your wildest desires and imagination. Come in, come in, and welcome." Ranny moves back. He's illuminated now by a thin, bright light coming from a slit of a window high in the castle.

"Did you ever read the Arthurian legends?" Ranny asks.

"Of course. That's why we wanted to come on this trip. Arthur represented all that was good and fine about England and knighthood," you say, unsure of what he's getting at.

Turn to page 71.

You dash for the oaken door and the bridge over the moat. You've got to get help!

Just as you finish squeezing through the crack in the door and under the huge, iron-toothed portcullis, it slams into place with a bone-crushing jolt.

"No!" you scream as one of the rusted iron teeth pierces your shirt. It misses your flesh by the barest inch. An inner voice screams at you to run but another voice, one of loyalty, screams equally loudly for you to go back and save Megan and Josh. *"Return,"* it says. "Return, before it's too late!"

You hesitate, take a deep breath, fight down your fear, and turn around. To your horror, the castle is fading! It's as if a giant eraser were smudging the edges and softening its shape and form. The two huge gargoyles on the oak door are growing dimmer. Maybe it's just the foggy mist, you think, rubbing your eyes. Or maybe it's your imagination.

Now you don't know *what* to do. Maybe you should stick around.

If you decide to stay, turn to page 75.

If you continue to flee, turn to page 16.

Finally, you stumble across the small cell. Megan is sitting on a tiny stool, her face streaked with tears. Rusted iron bars trap her, and a big, rusted padlock is clamped across the gate.

"I thought you'd never find me," she says, wiping her eyes. "I want out!"

"Okay, okay," you say, trying to think. You've got to get her out and get moving before Ranny finds you. Hurriedly, you start taking off your armor. It's hard work.

"There," you say, pulling off the last piece. Carefully, you take the breastplate and start hammering it into the lock.

Bam! Bam! The noise echoes throughout the gloomy corridors.

"Hurry up!" Megan whispers. "You've got to hurry!" She wrings her hands nervously.

"Maybe I can help you," says a small, bird-like voice.

"Huh?" you say, spinning around. Who spoke?

Turn to page 58.

"I'm ready," you reply.

Ranny leads you into a different part of the castle—you haven't been here before. You enter a large, high-ceilinged room hung with banners of red and gold silk embroidered with the heads of fantastical creatures—half dragon, half horse. Torches smolder in holders along the huge stone walls. Candles glow softly, and a large table stands in the center of the hall.

"Here," says Ranny, holding up a wrinkled piece of parchment and a pen. "Sign it."

You want to read it, but Ranny snatches it out of your grasp as soon as you've signed it. He points to the table. On it are two objects: a sword and a cup.

"Choose one. It will be your symbol," Ranny says, his voice firm and clear.

If you pick up the cup, turn to page 52.

If you select the sword, turn to page 57.

No good. They are still there, and so are you. The high stone walls of the castle enshroud you. The eyes of the knights gleam from behind the slits of their helmets. They look almost red. The once warm and gentle summer's night has become a chill and dank evening full of evil portents.

The silence is broken by the flapping of wings. You turn to see a raven settling on a niche of stone protruding from the south wall of the inner castle.

"So, you have made a wise decision. I applaud your courage," Ranny says, appearing out of the darkness. The two knights retreat. Again there is no clanking of their armor.

"What's going on?" you ask. You don't like this one bit.

"I have a proposition for you. You have two choices. We can play a little game I know. Or you can prepare yourself for a jousting tournament. Which do you choose?"

If you choose the game, turn to page 7.

If you decide to joust, turn to page 14.

40

"I told you not to come. I warned you," comes a voice. It is strained and heavy. Whoever is speaking sounds as if he is in pain.

Could it be the faceless knight of the note back home? Come on, you think, this isn't a TV show. This is the modern world, and things like ghosts and supernatural stuff don't really exist. Or do they?

"Scram! I'm tired. If it's you, Josh, you're in trouble—big time," you say. But you sound braver than you feel. You know it isn't Josh.

Turn to page 12.

Megan is chained to the wall. Both of her hands are shackled, and her back is pressed against the cold, hard stone.

"Megan! I'm here!" you yell, trying to run to her. The suit of armor weighs you down.

A one-armed man wearing a sackcloth shirt and trousers and carrying a rusted but nevertheless dangerous-looking ax rushes out to meet you. He swings; you duck. He swings again.

"Help!" Megan yells. "Get me down!"

But before you can do it, another creature, this time a beautiful woman, sweeps into the area with a large knife. She menaces you with it. You hope that your armor will protect you.

"Help!" Megan shouts again. "Get me down!"

Sword swipes fill the air.

The woman swishes the knife menacingly.

"Good! Good! I like it!" Ranny yells. "Save her, fool!"

You make a desperate lunge for Megan. But the floor is covered in slime, and you slip, falling hard.

Turn to page 66.

"Hey!" Megan's voice shouts out. "Save me! I'm over here, in a small cell."

You follow the voice, but it seems to move whenever you get near where it's coming from. You become frantic, running at full speed from voice to voice and bumping into walls and objects that feel like torture racks, cauldrons of hot oil, and collections of axes and ropes.

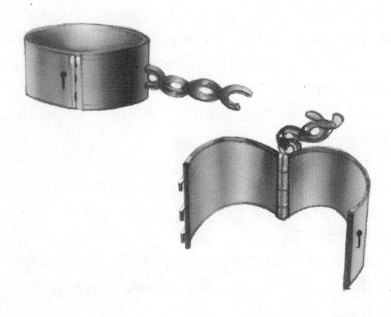

Turn to page 37.

You grab his hand. "I'm with you, Edmund." You turn to Megan. "Are you staying here?" you ask, motioning to her.

"Not!" she says, grabbing your other hand. "Let's go!" The three of you hurry down a dark corridor. It's funny—the rats seem to be staying out of Edmund's way, as if they know he's a ghost.

Every now and then you come across a torch that throws light your way. You notice that the prince's neck is red—as if he had been scratched with something.

"Have you, uh, been very successful in preventing further deaths here?" you ask nervously. "I'm just curious."

Prince Edmund nods, continuing to hurry along. "Yes, I've saved one or two."

"Out of how many?" asks Megan.

"Oh, about forty-nine."

You and Megan gasp.

"But I'm getting better," Prince Edmund continues. "I just rescued a boy your age. His name is Josh."

"Josh!" you yelp. "Where is he?"

Turn to page 72.

44

A cloud scuttles across the sky and obscures the moon for a few seconds. When the moon emerges from behind the cloud, there stands, as if by a conjurer's trick, the castle, huge and dark. It looks frightening.

From deep in the bowels of the castle comes what you think is a cry—a low-pitched, almost moaning sound. Could it be some strange type of owl or bird? Or is it the wind in some narrow passageway? But there is no wind, you realize. It must be your imagination.

"Come along, now, hurry. We're going to be late," the old man says.

"Late for what?" you ask.

Ranny smiles knowingly but does not speak.

You glance at Josh and Megan. They both seem fine. Maybe they don't hear the moaning. Your imagination must be running wild.

Ranny is leading you toward the back of the castle. The nearer you get to the old castle walls, the colder it gets, and a light wind picks up. Once again the moon is obscured by clouds. A light mist drizzles down on you.

Turn to page 50.

"Nestra!" you exclaim. Even though it's hard to see her, you'd recognize her voice anywhere. "What are *you* doing here?"

"I was trying to find the library, but I made a wrong turn and ended up down here," she says. "Do you know the way out?"

You shake your head. "No. But the guy who was giving us the tour turned out to be crazy. He's got Megan and Josh locked up somewhere!"

Nestra takes your hand. "Take me to him," she says. She sounds angry.

"You don't understand. He's nuts. And he's got some kind of power," you say.

Nestra starts walking in the direction you came from. "Come on," she says, ignoring your warning. In minutes you are back at the entrance. In the middle of the courtyard you see Ranny, polishing a suit of armor.

"Back so soon?" he says with an evil laugh. "Your friends will not be happy!" Then he sees Nestra behind you.

"Who is *that*?" he snarls, dropping the armor.

Turn to page 86.

46

"Get away from me!" you yell, threatening Ranny with the sword. It's a lot heavier than you'd expected.

You swing the sword in a broad arc, backing up into the corridor. Then you advance on the sounds of the struggle, sword held at the ready, eyes flashing.

The darkness of the corridor wraps you like a cloak, and the sounds of the struggle lead you deeper into the castle.

"I'm coming, Josh. I'm coming!" you shout. The sword gives you courage, and your blood runs hot. You grip the jeweled handle as though you had always had this weapon. It feels like a part of you: power, courage, might, victory.

The corridor broadens, and you see a light at the far end. Josh's screams and shouts lessen. There's a stairway before you, leading down, probably to the dungeons.

A hand reaches out, grasping for you. It seems to come from the stone wall, as though the stones were alive.

Turn to page 80.

"Ranny! Ranny!" you shout with all your might. "Come back!" You have a bad feeling about the old man, but he's the only person who can help you find your friends. "I want to talk with you!"

Silence. A wind nuzzles the castle walls and causes you to shiver.

"Ranny! Please!"

Still silence. You wonder if this is really part of the same twenty-four hours that started with a car trip to this old castle. It's been the longest day of your life.

The portcullis begins to ratchet back up, inch by inch. The sound is horrible. You can imagine your body pierced by the great rusty iron spikes. It takes three agonizing minutes for the portcullis to draw up. Placing your hands on the great wooden door, you slowly push it open and peer into the courtyard of the castle. There's no sign of your friends. Gray stone walls with slit windows, turrets, and a few small outbuildings for animals and food storage are all that meet your eyes.

Turn to page 27.

48

"Way to go, Megan!" you say, feeling a little twinge of jealousy that Megan won the contest and not you.

Josh coasts up on his BMX bike and pulls a wheelie just to show off. "Hey, did you hear about the trip?" he yells, hopping off his bike.

"What do you think?" you say.

"Don't diss me," Josh says. "Can you go?"

"When?" you ask excitedly.

"Next Tuesday," Megan says, holding out a sheaf of tickets in their red and blue holders. "We'll get to London in six hours. Then watch out, castles! My aunt Clytemnestra will meet us at the airport. She'll be our guardian. My mom already spoke to her. I hope your parents will let you go!"

It doesn't take much convincing to get your parents' approval. Megan's aunt Clytemnestra is a respected editor in an old English publishing house. She's very trustworthy.

The next few days are a blur of activity. First you need to get a special rush passport. And you have to decide what clothes to bring. You can't believe you're really going!

Turn to page 30.

50

"Hurry," the old man says again. He's walking very fast and urging the three of you on. "This is the Seventh Hundred!"

"The Seventh Hundred? What's that?" you ask.

"I thought you knew," Ranny replies. "You act as if you have been here before . . . long, long ago. Every hundred years the things that happened here seven hundred years ago are repeated. This time, I want to put an end to them. And you can help."

You don't like the sound of this one bit.

"What kinds of things?" Megan asks.

"Murder. Murder of the young prince of the castle. Murdered in his sleep. Head removed and never found again. That and the poisoning of the old man who watched the animals and trained the falcons. Other things too horrible to mention." The old man cackles in a way that reminds you of a cat toying with a mouse right before she bites its head off. Sometimes you wish you didn't have such an overactive imagination. Your mom says it's caused by eating too much sugar and chocolate.

Turn to page 84.

You hurry down winding, narrow steps that lead you further into the gloomy depths of the castle. Slime coats the walls and rats are scurrying about. "Ugh!" you gasp, as a stench like the bathrooms at school at the end of the day hits your nose. This is the real thing! This is a dungeon.

Slowly, you feel your way along the slimy walls. "Megan?" you whisper, lifting up the faceplate of your helmet "Are you down here?" As you speak, a rat runs underneath your foot, startling you. You're glad that you're still wearing armor, so your body doesn't have to touch anything.

"Pssst! Can you hear me?" you hiss.

Then you hear something.

Turn to page 42.

52

Despite the fact that the sword attracts you, you overcome your taste for violence and move instinctively for the cup. Your hand reaches out.

"Drats! Not the cup again!" Ranny shouts, lunging for you. "I hate people who take the cup and leave the sword! I hate them with the power of the three newts, the seven pikes, and the eyes of a snake! Curses on you!"

Ranny snatches at the cup, but you are quicker and grab it just in time. The cup glows, as if it were radioactive. The warmth coming from it fills you with a strange, unearthly energy.

"Be gone, Ranny, or whoever you are," you hear yourself say. "The world has had enough of the likes of you. *Curses* on curses. Let the past be and get on with life! The Seventh Hundred is in your mind, not in our lives!"

Ranny jumps back, his wrinkled face a mixture of fear and hatred. He reaches into his cloak and withdraws a small crystal bottle.

Turn to page 6.

Ranny laughs. "A deal? What kind of a deal could you make that I might need? You have nothing to deal with. I'm in command here, and I need new people for my dungeons." You gasp, your stomach churning with fear. "You and your friends happen to be those new people. The Seventh Hundred approaches." Ranny turns and recedes into the depths. The iron gate with its wicked points begins its slow descent.

"Unless . . . ," Ranny says slowly, still moving away, "you would be willing to work for me."

"What?" you exclaim. You can't believe what you're hearing. "Work for you? What could I possibly do for you?"

"Deliver others to me for my dungeons. If you do, I'll let your friends go. Think about it."

If you pretend to give in, turn to page 34.

If you make a dash and try to get back out again, turn to page 67.

Tommy holds a small flashlight in his hand. He leads the way to a secret tunnel that goes under the dining room and emerges in a sub-basement filled with cobwebs, heaps of ancient trash, and some strange, unidentifiable shapes.

"My mom hates to come down here," Tommy tells you. "She says it's too creepy and dark." He pulls a spider from one of the webs and flings it at you. *"Bahhh!"* he yells, laughing when he sees your face.

Finally you emerge into the true basement, where the castle's dungeons are found. A single electric bulb illuminates the cavernous, rocky space whose shadows work upon your imagination.

"That's not very funny," you say, watching the spider crawl down your leg and onto the floor.

Tommy makes a face. "Can't you take a joke?" he asks.

"Sure I can," you say. "Throwing spiders isn't my idea of a joke."

Turn to page 23.

56

You decide to stay with Nestra. The old man looks disappointed but agrees to meet Megan and Josh at eight P.M.

Ravensford Castle is more than eight hundred years old. Last year, new owners had purchased the castle, and they needed to raise money to keep it afloat. So they turned one of the castle's wings into a bed-and-breakfast.

"Welcome to Ravensford Castle," says a pleasant woman behind a small wooden desk. "I'm the owner, Mrs. Findley."

"We're the contest winners!" Megan tells her.

Mrs. Findley smiles. "Of course! I was expecting you. You'll have our best rooms!" Megan high-fives you and Josh.

After Nestra fills out the necessary paperwork, Mrs. Findley leads you up a wide staircase to the second floor. You pass by vases of fresh flowers, mirrors trimmed with gold, and even a suit of armor.

"Wow," says Megan, reaching out to touch it. "Is it real?"

"Yes," says Mrs. Findley.

"Can we get inside it?" Josh asks.

Turn to page 11.

"The sword. I select the sword," you say, going along with him. "But what about my friends?" The glittering sword's handle is topped by a large crystal. Could it be a diamond?

"Good choice. Pick it up," Ranny says, ignoring your question.

You hesitate and then reach out tentatively. The sword seems to give off an energy, a vibration that is both powerful and warm. Closer you reach, closer, until . . .

"Don't do it!" a voice screams from the gloom of the corridor that leads away from the great hall. "Don't touch it!" It's Josh!

Ranny reacts with sudden anger and violence. "Finish him off!" he screams into the darkness. The sound of a struggle erupts from the corridor.

"Josh! I'm coming!" you shout, running for your friend.

Ranny screams and lunges for you. He manages to grab your shirt and pull you to a halt. Filled with rage, you swivel until you are only a foot from the table.

In a flash you pick up the sword.

Turn to page 46.

58

There, standing behind your discarded armor, is a small boy. He looks about seven or eight years old. His hair is flaxen, and his eyes are watery and green. Gently, he touches your shoulder.

"Who are you?" you shriek, falling against the bars. Megan's eyes are wide.

"I am Prince Edmund," the boy says softly. "I was murdered here many, many years ago." He's wearing dark green leggings and a soft, silky shirt buttoned up to his neck.

"Well, what are you doing here now?" Megan asks, peering down at him. "Are you a ghost?"

"The old man who roams these dungeons is a descendant of my murderer. It is my hope to stop any further deaths from occurring," Prince Edmund says. Stepping forward, he takes the rusted padlock in his hands. As if by magic, the lock disintegrates into dust.

"Whoa . . . ," you say. "How did you—"

"Please. Follow me. It is your only chance of getting out alive."

If you decide to follow Prince Edmund, turn to page 43.

If you want to think it over, turn to page 73.

Something rubs against you. You reach out, and it is not there. You see a white, gauzy image of a woman with tears in her eyes.

"Leave before it's too late," she whispers. "Let me help you." She pulls off your helmet. Your face is red and sweaty, and your hair is sticking to your forehead. The woman helps you pull off your gloves and breastplate. Soon, you're standing there in just your regular clothes.

"Now go!" says the woman, fading away.

You feel strange without the armor. Light and airy, as if you just lost a hundred pounds. Well, you think, you did!

You're so glad to have the armor off, you jump into the air. "Yeah!" you shout. The vibration of your jump causes a block of stone to loosen on one of the vaulted arches above you. It teeters ever so slightly.

"Watch out!" yells a vaguely familiar voice as the large stone breaks free. It's too late. The stone falls with crushing impact upon your body.

The End

60

Must be the wind, you decide, returning to your seat on the couch. You continue to flip through the book. You come to a chapter of portraits. First there is a blank page, with the numbers "1295." On the next page is a portrait. "Prince Edmund, 1286–1295. Beheaded, Ravensford Castle," reads the type under a picture of a small blond boy.

"That's here!" you exclaim. The painting is different from the other ones you've seen. It looks so real, almost like a photograph.

The next page reads "1395," and is followed by a portrait of a young woman in a long green gown. "Lady Anne, 1375–1395. Drowned, Ravensford Castle," reads the type underneath. It startles you. *Another murder. Exactly one hundred years later!*

A slight wave of fear washes over you. Tentatively, you turn to the next page. "1495." This is followed by a painting of another death—in 1495. And again in 1595. You realize that terrible deaths have occurred every hundred years at Ravensford Castle.

Turn to page 85.

"Harder!" shouts the knight.

You gulp and give a firmer tug. Pull, pull, pull—there! The helmet comes flying off, and you go flying backward, landing with a thud on your back.

You're almost afraid to look. Slowly, you rise to face the faceless knight.

But he's not faceless. In fact, he has one of the roundest, reddest, and most exasperated faces you've ever seen.

"I *tried* to tell my wife that this would *not* be a fun experience. But no. She had to talk me into putting on this silly knight outfit and pretending I'm King Arthur or something. We just about scared some people to death back behind the castle—even the old man who works here ran and hid. Then we got separated." He shakes his head. "Some vacation! Can you help me up, kid?"

Sighing with relief, you nod. So much for knights in shining armor! you think.

The End

62

Before your amazed eyes, two large horses are brought into the courtyard by a knight in full armor. One of the horses is red and the other is black. Another faceless knight brings two lances. Ranny hands a suit of armor to you. With great difficulty, you put it on. First the chain mail, which is very heavy, then the breastplate, and then the greaves, which go below your knees. Good thing you know where all this stuff goes, since Ranny isn't helping you at all. Then the gauntlets, and finally, the helmet.

"Good," Ranny shouts with glee. "You look like a proper knight. But there are other problems for you to worry about right now. Pay attention. I want you to be one of my best pupils. Look over there!"

You freeze where you are and turn around.

Turn to page 41.

After you check in, Mrs. Findley, the proprietor of the castle, takes you up to your rooms. You and Josh each have your own room, while Megan is sharing with Nestra. The rooms are nice-sized, and you even have your own fireplace. You unpack your things and then head down to the castle's dining room for dinner. There are a few other diners besides you four. The food is plain, but good.

"It's seven fifty," says Megan, looking at her watch. She pushes her half-eaten pudding out of the way. "Let's go!"

"Go along, dears," says Nestra. "But be careful." Nestra has asked Mrs. Findley about the old man—Mrs. Findley says he's rather eccentric but harmless. And a great gardener.

"I'll just catch up on my reading a bit," Nestra says.

You, Josh, and Megan walk down the gloomy dark hallway and push open the castle door. The full moon splashes the landscape with light. You stand there waiting.

"Where is he?" you mutter. "It's eight-oh-two."

"Be patient," says Megan. "He said he'd be here."

Turn to page 9.

64

You make your decision to stay and face the knights and whatever lies deep within this castle in the twinkling of an eye. Maybe this is just some kind of joke Ranny is playing on you.

One of your favorite stories is the legend of King Arthur. You love reading about Merlin, the magician who practiced white magic. Often Merlin would do strange things more as jokes than to harm anyone. Maybe Ranny is like Merlin. On the other hand, he could be a practitioner of black magic. In that case, you, Josh, and Megan are probably doomed.

The great iron portcullis slams its giant teeth down on the threshold. There is no chance for escape now. The knights have stopped advancing and stand mute and ominous in front of you. This is not like the books you love to read so much. This is real. Or is it? You are badly confused. Is this a dream? Have you entered a world of imagination? Can you retreat with the snap of a finger?

Snap! You snap your fingers, trying to will yourself out of the situation.

Turn to page 39.

"Good question," Ranny replies. "It depends upon how much I decide to torture them. I'll give you a break. I'll be really fair and only make them suffer a little to begin with. Later on, in the second round—if there *is* a second round—the pain might get worse and more difficult to stop."

You are horrified. This evil little man is toying with your friends' lives the way a kid plays with toy soldiers or dolls or trucks.

Ranny steps back. "Seek!" he announces. You dart through a small door that leads into the castle, and find yourself in a narrow passageway. It seems like the passageway is going around the castle's perimeter, but you can't be sure.

"Josh! Megan! I'm coming!" you yell. You feel the blood surge in your veins—just thinking about your friends gives you courage. You've got to find them—time is running out.

Turn to page 26.

66

Reaching up, you manage to grab Megan and break the old rusted cuffs that hold her to the wall. She falls with a thump to the floor.

"Let's go!" you say. But there is no response.

"Megan! Megan!" you shout in vain.

That's when you realize that it's not Megan. It's a life-size dummy that looks like her. Somehow Ranny fooled you with a tape of her voice.

"This way!" Josh shouts from high above. You can't see him, but you can make out a stairway leading to the upper reaches of the castle.

"No! *This* way!" comes Megan's voice. It seems to be coming from below, where the dungeons are. The one-armed man and the beautiful woman stand there eyeing you, weapons in their hands.

You don't know what to do. It's obvious that Ranny can use your friends' voices to fool you. But what if it really *is* them screaming?

If you decide to trust Megan, turn to page 51.

If you want to go to help Josh—if it is Josh—turn to page 22.

The door is starting to shut. In desperation, you squeeze through. "Please! Please help me, sombody, please!" you shout through lips dry with fear. The door is pressing against you, wedging you between it and the portcullis, which is steadily coming down.

You bend down to squeeze under the jaws of the portcullis. Once you're free, maybe you can get help from Nestra or one of the dining room cooks or waiters. Or maybe you can hide somewhere in the woods and wait until morning, when it will be easier to find your way back to the front entrance.

It seems almost impossible. The door is pushing against your back—and the portcullis is only a foot from the ground. Squatting, you try to crawl—*Squash!* All at once, the portcullis comes slamming down, and the door is pushed completely shut. You are squished between the rusted iron spikes and the wooden door, your face squished up against the cold bars. Your pleas for help go unanswered. The pressure against your chest is unbearable. As you gasp for air, your last thoughts are of your friends, and then of home and school and skateboarding. Then . . . blackness.

The End

"We're not going anywhere, Ranny," you say, deciding to call his bluff. "You have no powers over us or over anyone. This is all a sham, a mean joke. We're going to call in the authorities. Believe me, messing with Americans is no joke," you add hotly.

"That's right," says Megan. The two of you join hands with Josh. Nothing happens, to your relief. Ranny rears back on his heels and laughs a hollow, horrible laugh that is half cough, half death rattle.

"People have done that before. Fat lot of good it did them. I've got plenty more room here for you. You're wrong. And I'm right. Watch this!"

He raises his hands, grasps a large rope that hangs from the ceiling, and tugs.

You look up. A large trapdoor in the ceiling opens. Before you can move, a wrought-iron cage comes sailing down.

You, Josh, and Megan are trapped. Ranny has you. . . .

The End

"Uh . . . no. Who's that?"

"Mrs. Findley's son. He's just about your age. He's usually out and about—maybe you'll run into him tomorrow."

"Sounds good," you say. You always like to meet new people. You give Nestra a smile.

"I'm going to go into the library for a while," you tell her. She's struck up a conversation with another guest. "I'm in the mood for a good book."

The library is located in the south corner of the castle. It's fairly small, but the walls are brimming with books. Most look old, almost as old as the castle. There are a few hard leather couches, and some dust-covered tables. Thick green velvet curtains frame the windows.

"Hmmm," you say, thumbing through the shelves. Nothing really catches your eye. Then you come across a book about medieval art and knights. It looks interesting, even though it's very old. The binding practically falls apart in your hands.

"Guess this will have to do," you say, plopping down on one of the couches.

Turn to page 25.

"Very good, my young friend. Very good. Then you understand that within good there is also the potential for evil. Well, we will witness that tonight." He gives you a pat on the back as though you have been a good dog. You recoil from his touch, and he chuckles knowingly.

"What about my friends? You said they would go free and unharmed."

"Don't worry. I am good to my word. But first, are you willing to sign a pact?"

Turn to page 38.

Prince Edmund smiles. "I believe he is sitting in the kitchen of the castle, drinking tea and telling his story to your friend's aunt."

All of a sudden you hear a loud howl. Prince Edmund's face tightens with fear, and he rubs his neck. "Come. You must hurry. I will fade away if I come in contact with the old man. The power of my murderer has been passed down to him," he says.

Down one corridor after another you run, cobwebs sticking to your face and hands. You think you may even have been nipped by a rat, but there's no time to stop.

"How can you see?" pants Megan, trying to catch her breath. "I can't see anything."

"Shhh!" says Prince Edmund. You feel his small, cold hand tense. "I hear something." Then a cackling laugh breaks the silence.

"I'm coming!" It's Ranny! His voice doesn't sound that far away. "You'll pay dearly for this, my little American friends! With your heads!"

Turn to page 82.

"I—I don't know," you stutter, your eyes darting from Megan to the small boy. "How do we know you're telling the truth?"

Megan nods. "Maybe it's a trick!"

The small boy smiles sadly. "Your doubting nature will cost you dearly. I must go." As if by magic, he disappears.

"We should have gone with him!" Megan cries. "He *was* going to help us!"

You throw your hands into the air. "Well how was I—"

Bam! Something big and heavy hits you on the head. Slowly, you slide to the ground.

When you awake, you find yourself alone in a small cell. There is a calendar on the wall. It runs for one hundred years—and there is a red pencil hanging on a string next to it to mark each one off.

Desperately, you search for a way out. But there is none. One thing is certain: You'll have plenty of time to prepare for the coming of the Eighth Hundred.

The End

"I can't believe we get to stay here for free," says Josh, as Nestra slowly drives up the twisting road. The castle looms in front of you—huge, turreted, dark, remote, and cold.

Nestra pulls into a parking spot. You all get out of the car and begin to get your bags. An old man trimming a giant bush on the side of the castle beckons to you.

"Moonlit nights are the best time to see the old castle. Tonight will be perfect," he says, pointing up to the sky. Even though it isn't dark yet, the moon is visible. "I'll show you around," he says. "I actually live here." His eyes are bright and friendly. His left hand is shriveled and twisted, and his shoulders are bowed by the years.

"Well, I don't know . . . ," says Nestra. She looks skeptical. "I'm tired. And we've got to check in. Let's do it tomorrow."

The old man squints at you with a knowing look. "I won't be here tomorrow." He turns and starts to walk away but then stops. "The dungeons here are very interesting, especially on full-moon nights," he says. "There's one in particular you'd like." He nods at you.

Turn to page 8.

"Stop!" you yell with all your might. "Stop, I tell you!"

But the castle keeps fading. From deep within its walls comes the thin silver voice of Josh in agony.

"H . . . el . . . lllllllllllp!"

Your heart feels like it's going to burst. Your blood solidifies like Silly Putty. You can't leave them.

"I'm coming!" you scream. You search your memory for stories of old castles and their curses. You remember one castle that was supposed to appear every hundred years, just for a night. But that was just a fairy tale, wasn't it?

You wish that this were all a dream and that you were back home. But you're not. Like it or not, you're thousands of miles away. Maybe you *are* facing the Seventh Hundred, the anniversary of murder and treachery.

The castle has stopped disappearing. It stands large and remote, forbidding and powerful.

Turn to page 47.

76

All of a sudden a knight, dressed in full battle armor, comes flying out of the fog, straight at you. His horse is bucking wildly.

"Oh!" you shriek, half in fear, half in awe. You're not sure if it's one of the knights you saw in the courtyard or not. It's hard to tell. They all have the same metal faces. You've always dreamt about knights, and now you're only a few feet away from one. But you aren't prepared for battle!

The knight seems just as startled as you are. To your surprise, he seems a bit shaky. Reaching out to grab on to the horse, he loses his balance and topples off.

Crash! The armor makes a horrible banging as it smashes onto the ground. The horse turns and gallops away.

"Please, don't hurt me," you whisper, backing up. "I . . . I didn't mean to frighten your horse. I'm kind of lost, and I was—"

"Don't just stand there, help me!" shouts the knight. "Get this thing off my head!"

Shaking, you move forward and place your hands on the metal helmet. It's ice-cold. Carefully, you pull.

Turn to page 61.

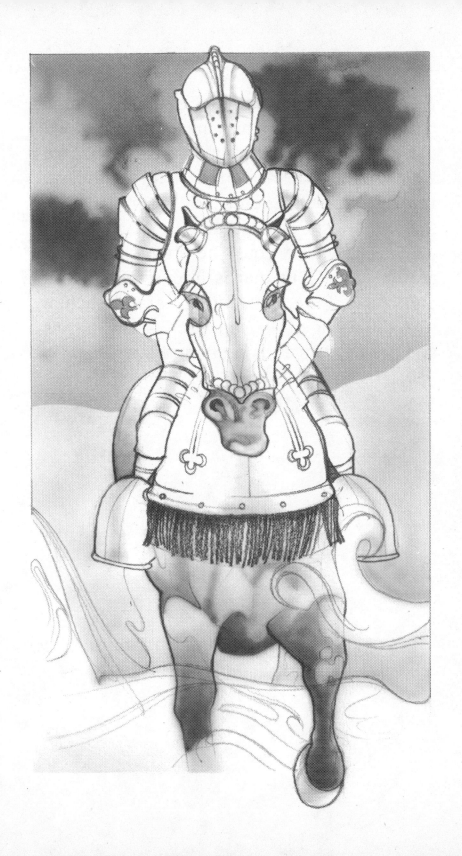

78

Finally, with a combined effort, all four of you gain the window and make the long fall to the moat with a minimum of fuss. With foresight, Archibald has removed his armor, revealing that he is a young boy, not much older than you, Josh, and Megan.

"Take me with you!" he shouts once you are on shore. But that is impossible, for the end of the Seventh Hundred is approaching with the rising of the sun. Archibald vanishes, and the castle stands mute and large.

The End

"How did you get to know about us?" you ask, mystified by this new development. After all, you are in England, and you know no one here except Nestra.

"E-mail! Simple, really. I communicate with a group of American kids who love castles and knights and all the stuff you and your friends are into. You contacted them about joining, then they contacted us. We thought we'd work out a little surprise for you, so we wrote the note and sent it on your E-mail address. It's all good fun, you know. No harm meant. I live here. My mom runs the castle."

"Ohhh . . . ," you say. "You're Tommy Findley!"

Tommy smiles and slaps you on the back. "You got it!"

"What's next?" you ask, your heartbeat returning to normal.

"Well, we've arranged a tour of the castle. There's a myth about it celebrating a hundred-year anniversary. Tonight is the Seventh Hundred."

Turn to page 87.

"No!" you shout, slashing with your mighty sword and severing the arm from the wall. The disembodied arm falls to the floor and disappears. You hear Ranny's laughter.

"Good! Good for you!" Ranny says. "Follow your anger. Use your sword."

You barely hear Ranny's words. The steps lead downward steeply. Your heart is racing.

Two steps. Another two. Then three. The walls reach out again, and you force your way through a forest of stretching, grabbing arms and hands. The threat of the sword does its work.

The steps end, and a small, cramped space illuminated by a single candle reveals eleven people chained to the wall. Some are old, some skeletons, some young. In the middle of the far wall are Josh and Megan. Their chains are shiny and new and their faces are filled with terror.

Raising your sword, you enter the room, ready for a fight. Seeing that the coast is clear, you run over to your friends.

Turn to page 31.

"I don't know! I noticed this trapdoor beneath me." He points down to a small handle on the floor. "And when I bent down to pull it, this cord wrapped around my ankle!"

"We'll cut it!" You want out of this weird place!

"No!" Megan says, gripping your hand and holding it away from the silver cord. "What if it grabs you, too?"

"I'm afraid you are being too hasty," Ranny says, emerging from the stairway behind you. "If Josh cuts the cord, he dies."

"You are evil," you say to Ranny.

"Perhaps, but I hold the key to your freedom."

"What is it?" Josh asks.

"The key to your freedom lies in your contacting the World of the Dead for me."

"Why us, Ranny? Why not you?" you ask.

Ranny runs a cold finger across your cheek. "I have used up my visits. If I go back, I'll have to stay."

"But you're practically dead right now," Josh mutters.

"Not quite," Ranny says.

Turn to page 68.

"We're almost there," the prince tells you. He's still holding your hand, but his other hand has wrapped itself around his neck. You come to a crashing halt in front of a tiny spiral staircase. "Here. Run up this stairway, through the room it leads to, and you will find safety. Hasten!"

"But what about you? Isn't Ranny—"

Edmund pushes you toward the stairs. *"Go!"*

Without another word, you and Megan scramble up the stairs. At the top, you find a trapdoor. "Hurry!" Megan shrieks, pushing past you and shoving with all her might against the door. It pops open, and you and she leap into the room, slamming the trapdoor down behind you. In the distance below, you hear the muffled screams of Prince Edmund.

Racing through the dark room, you burst through double doors on the far side.

"What in the world?" cries a maid, dropping a dustcloth from her hands.

You look around you. Carpeted floors, vases with fresh flowers . . . you're safe!

Turn to page 88.

"Lead the way," Josh says. It figures. He is always ready to get everybody into trouble.

You had thought there was only one entrance to the castle. But here, in the back, is another. You watch as Ranny strides forward.

Bbrrrrrrrrrrr. Clunkkkkkk. Bbrrrrrrrrrrrr.

The sound in your ears is like a huge saw blade rubbed by a wooden pole! But it's only the noise made by the portcullis rising and a huge oaken door swinging just wide enough for a person to enter. Far back in the rear courtyard of the castle you see a flickering light, probably from a candle. Suddenly it goes out.

"Well, here we are, then. Welcome to the dungeons of Ravensford Castle." Ranny seems to have taken added strength from being near the dungeons. He walks a little straighter, and his back seems less humped. His smile is wider and his teeth a touch brighter.

"Nice, very nice," you muster. It's certainly different from the *front* of the castle.

Turn to page 20.

You continue to turn the pages. To your surprise, you come to "1995." How can that be? Has someone been murdered at the castle this year? Wouldn't you have heard about it? You feel very uneasy. With a heavy hand, you turn the page.

There is a painting of a child about eleven years old, dressed in modern-day clothes. The child's face is smiling. Below it, the type reads "Tourist, 1984–1995. Information to come."

The book falls with a heavy thud to the ground. A piercing chill sweeps through your numb body.

The child is you.

The End

"I want those children back now!" Nestra says. To your astonishment, Ranny actually looks afraid of her.

"It was just a little game," he whispers. "Just a game." He dashes down the narrow steps that lead to the dungeons below. In minutes, Josh and Megan come tearing up the stairs.

"Guys!" you shout, flinging your arms around them. "Are you okay?"

"Yeah. Just hungry," says Josh.

"Let's go!" you say, peering into the darkness. "Ranny might come back!"

Nestra shakes her head. "I don't think so. He knows I mean business."

Megan laughs. "See?" she says. "I told you she was cool!"

The End

"What kind of anniversary?" you ask.

"This castle has seen many things, both good and bad. According to the myth, tonight's an anniversary of bad things that repeat themselves every hundred years. The legend is pretty much a tourist thing. But—you never know." Tommy grins at you.

"So, we'll meet in the morning," you say, eyeing your pillow hopefully.

"Oh, no. It has to be tonight," Tommy says. "Nothing ever happens during the day."

"Well . . . okay," you say. "Just let me get dressed first."

You get dressed and, with a growing sense of excitement, join Tommy in the hallway. E-mail has gotten you into some pickles before, but that's another story for another time.

Josh and Megan are sleeping. They had fun before . . . now it's your turn, you decide. And *snooze, you lose* is one of your favorite expressions.

Turn to page 55.

After the maid calms you both down, she hurries to get Nestra and Mrs. Findley. You tell them your story. Nestra looks doubtful—but Mrs. Findley looks very serious.

"And the poor prince! Can't we help him?" Megan asks.

"Show me the trapdoor," Mrs. Findley says, walking into the room you came from.

"Sure, it's right—" You stop. The door is gone!

Mrs. Findley puts her hands on your shoulder. "I didn't want to frighten you when you arrived. But this has happened before. The little prince was indeed murdered here seven hundred years ago. And other guests have seen his ghost wandering the halls."

"How did he die?" you ask.

"Beheaded," she says sadly.

"What about Ranny?" you ask. "You told us it was okay to go with him."

Mrs. Findley's face pales. "I said it was all right to go with our gardener. But his name isn't Ranny. It's Gilbert. Ranny is the name of the executioner from seven hundred years ago!"

The End